a trainful of strangers

eleanor hull

a trainful of strangers

drawings by joan sandin

atheneum   1968   new york

to

TAMARA & VINCENT WRIGHT

for whom

the city holds no strangers

Copyright © 1968 by Eleanor Hull
All rights reserved
Library of Congress catalog card number 68-18449
Published simultaneously in Canada by
McClelland & Stewart, Ltd.
Manufactured in the United States of America
Printed by Halliday Lithograph Corporation,
West Hanover, Massachusetts
Bound by The Book Press, Inc.,
Brattleboro, Vermont
Designed by Judith Lerner
First Edition

contents

a trainful of
strangers

a train to
wherever it goes

DOBBS HENRY WOKE UP and then wished he hadn't.
School.

Every day he opened his eyes and saw the crack
in the ceiling above him and smelled the coffee and
grits and heard his mother's voice scolding the twins
in and out of the bathroom. Every day he pulled the
covers up over his face to delay having to come out
—out of the bed onto the splintery floor, out of the
apartment into the dark smelly hallway, out of the
hallway into the mess and noise of the street, out of
the rush and crowd into the unfriendly sternness of
Public School 39, and that box in a box, Homeroom 6.

He could see Miss Frimmer's fierce smile as she
held up the word chart and pointed at him. "Are you
ready, Dobbs Henry? I'm sure you're ready today."

But he wasn't.

S-l-a-t-e and t-a-l-e-s; the same letters jumbled around every which way; and one was slate and the other was tales, but he didn't know why. In order to hide how stupid he was, Dobbs Henry would shrug, make a face, and pretend he didn't care.

After English came Social Studies, and in that class they were putting on plays. First they had studied the Indians, and some bashful girl he'd never noticed before turned out to be part Indian, and had to stand around and be the main character while the Pilgrims landed, barking their shins on the wooden shore.

Then there were Spanish explorers; how the two Puerto Rican kids strutted! But their cardboard swords were real funny; they wouldn't have scared an old lady.

And now they had got to the Negroes.

Miss Frimmer took on about what she called "Negro History." She told them about John Henry, a steelworker in the olden times, who drove a spike into a rock with a hammer faster than a steam drill could do it, and then died.

"Great," James said out loud in class.

Miss Frimmer pretended not to hear and went on about Sojourner Truth—who sounded interesting at first, but turned out to be only a lady lecturer whose real name was Isabella—and Benjamin Banneker, a mathematician. Dobbs Henry couldn't get too much excited. They were dead. And the live ones, those athletes and all, were nothing but pictures to him.

Then there was Lab, where they learned from Mr. Levy how to do experiments. That was pretty good. Everybody had a chance. But Dobbs Henry could never watch Mr. Levy's swift brown hands setting up the experiments without being thrown by the scar on the back of the right hand. That came from the time when James had switched bottles in the chemical rack. Dobbs Henry hadn't thought up the plan or carried it out, either, but he'd stood quiet and watched with his mouth wide open while James did it. It didn't seem like just switching bottles was so bad—but it was. Mr. Levy was the only one who got hurt, though.

At first Mr. Levy's hand was bandaged, then it came out in the open with a red puckered seam across the back. Now the scar was fading out some, but it would always be there. So Lab was just one of the things Dobbs Henry dreaded, and had to go through every day.

Almost every day. All of a sudden Dobbs Henry, still lying on the bed, noticed that things were very quiet. No voices, no "Hurry up, Sophronia! Take care, Appolonia!"

No, "Aw, Mama, let me be!" "Make *her* hurry!"

No smell of coffee.

It was Saturday!

Dobbs Henry got limp with relief. He could turn over and go to sleep again. He flopped onto his stomach, scratching himself on the wire that poked up from the springs through the pad of old comforts that served as a mattress. He sagged and stretched luxuriously and waited for sleep to drop gently around him again.

But it was too late. He was too wide awake. He got to wondering what Mama would have cooked up for him to do. She was always planning, cleaning, fixing. When she complained about the plaster falling, the landlord said it was because she washed the walls too often.

"You're hard on the place, Mrs. Morton," said the landlord sadly. "You wear stuff out."

"So give me some paint, and I'll cover up the holes," she answered instantly.

The landlord said he would, and continued to say so every other Saturday when he came to collect the rent. But the last few times, Mama hadn't been able to pay him.

"You know very well I won't cheat you, Mr. Maus," Mama said, looking straight at him, with her arms crossed on her chest. "It's just that my husband ain't been able to send a check for two months, and the Welfare ain't got around to supplementing yet."

The landlord waved his hands in the air. "Why I

ever take in Welfare clients I don't know!"

"I know," said Mama. "It because you gets paid more regular than by the others, who is liable to lose their jobs any time. And you'll get paid this time, too; just hold back them galloping horses."

And the landlord left, but he didn't say anything that time about the paint, and Mama didn't either.

Was this the Saturday the landlord would come again? Dobbs Henry was pretty sure the money hadn't come yet from either Daddy or the Welfare.

He raised himself up cautiously so as not to make the springs squeak. He'd better get away while the getting was good. He sure didn't want to stick around for that landlord bit.

He might have made it if he hadn't opened the refrigerator.

"Dobbs Henry!"

He held his breath.

"You gone? You not gone, I hear the door squeak! Don't you sneak out, now!"

"Why can't I go, Mama? It Saturday!"

"Ain't you going to that picnic at the church?"

"I don't want to go to no picnic at the church. It's for the little kids."

"They got a section for junior highs, if you too big for your grade—like you *are*."

Mama was always after him for not being smart.

"Besides," she said, and he could hear her getting out of bed, "I got things around the house for you to do."

If he was ever going to leave, he'd have to do it before she came out and looked at him. He shoved his toes into his shoes, grabbed a hunk of pork out of a bowl of greens from last night, and with the grease dripping down his sleeve, and his untied shoes slapping, beat it out the door.

James was waiting for him, leaning against a lamppost as if he just happened to be there. As soon as Dobbs Henry came out on the stoop, James started to stroll away.

"Hey, James, wait a minute!"

Dobbs Henry wiggled his heels down the best he could (the counters were broken) and tried to tie the frayed shoelaces and hop along at the same time. He never could quite believe James meant to let him go along.

"Whereat we going, James?"

"Whereat?" James repeated. "Whereat we going? Who knows?" He cocked his elbows and turned out his toes. "I don't know about you, but me, I plan to hop down in that subway and take me a train to wherever it goes!"

—Like the dirty old subway could just take off, like a plane or a bird, and go wherever it wanted!

"Who you kidding, wherever it goes!" said Dobbs Henry. "You know where it goes, and you got an idea!"

He wiped his greasy fingers on the back of his pants and caught up with James at the steps to the subway.

the outsiders

SUSAN CREPT DOWN the stairs, peering over the bannister into the dining room.

Her long neck stretched out like a giraffe as she tried to make her getaway, Susan thought, swallowing a giggle that threatened to choke her.

She could see Mother and Daddy at the breakfast table, alternately lecturing away at Hal, who was twisting his feet around the chair legs in his nervous eagerness to escape.

If she could get out the front door without their noticing her, she would call, "Come on, Hal! It's time to go!" and run ahead down the walk. They would all jump up and pursue her, but maybe she could get away before Mother noticed her hair.

Susan opened the door and, with her hand still on the knob, called back, "Hal! Hurry up! It's time—"

And, crash! Her right foot, on the skating board somebody'd left on the porch, spun out from under her and she thundered down on the sooty porch floor.

She was struggling up in a minute, in spite of a maddening pain in her knee, but Mother and Daddy and Hal were all upon her.

"What in the world!" Daddy fumed, shaking her gently to test her connections. "Are you trying to kill yourself?"

"Baby, are you hurt?" moaned Mother, leaning over to examine the banged-up knee.

"I told you to put that skating board away when you were through with it," said Hal.

Then they looked at her.

The whole family did a double take when it dawned on them that their despised little sister had become a great beauty, Susan thought, swallowing another giggle because they looked so funny, even if it meant the end of her new hairdo.

"Susan! You weren't going downtown with your hair like that!"

So she had to limp upstairs and comb it all out.

"That's so much better," said Mother when she came back down. "Now you look like the nice, wholesome little girl you are. Does your leg still hurt?"

"Not my leg," sighed Susan.

Mother looked promptingly at Daddy, who said,

"Susan, since Hal has to keep track of the trains and the fares and all, why don't you handle the tickets to the TV show?"

Big deal! this was to make up to her for her calamity and their insults. Transparent!

"Oh, I better put them in my pocket," said Hal. "You know how she is, she might—"

Susan grabbed the tickets and shoved them in her sweater pocket. "—lose them," she finished for him, and stalked down the sidewalk, speeding up every time Hal almost caught her. They were both running by the time they reached the corner, which was a good thing, since otherwise they would have missed the bus.

"You're even late on Saturday!" teased the bus driver.

Susan smiled and stuck out her tongue at him. She sat down, but Hal ignored the empty place beside her and sat behind.

O.K., O.K., she didn't want to sit with the jerk anyway.

But when the bus began filling up, Susan flipped around and sat beside him. She didn't want to get trapped among strangers. Hal was the one who knew the way, because Dad had taken him down on the subway last Saturday just to be sure. And he was sixteen months older, which right now made him twelve while she was still ten. And she had to have *somebody* to talk to.

"The cars look like a herd of animals stampeding by, don't they?" she said.

"They don't look like animals at all," said Hal, after considering. "You don't even think so yourself —you just like to say funny things."

Susan sighed. As usual, her idea fell to pieces when Hal attacked it. The cars *had* reminded her of a stampeding herd in a TV Western; but actually, cattle tossed their horns and plunged around a lot. Now she realized that the rigid colored shells of the cars made them more resemble a horde of beetles. But she wouldn't tell Hal.

The bus turned onto the Thruway. The towers of the city loomed beyond the park, floating on morning mist (or smog), and looking farther off and taller than they really were, than any real towers could be.

"I can't believe it!" Susan said, her feelings boiling over again. "Just us, going to New York by ourselves! What an adventure!"

"It's not an adventure," said Hal. "It's real. It's Science. I don't see what you're going for; girls aren't interested in Science."

"They are too!" said Susan indignantly. She thought about it. She wasn't, really. But she could be if she wanted to. It was just that there were so many more interesting things to be interested in.

Anyway, Science Searchlight wasn't just Science, it was a TV Show. Susan had never seen a TV Show in person.

The bus pulled up at the subway station and honked madly at a shiny black car that had stopped to drop somebody off. It dropped a boy off.

"Oh, look, there's John Kent Haven!" said Susan.

"Being hand-delivered by his Mommy," agreed Hal.

The long train, jointed like a caterpillar, waited at the top of the long iron staircase. It panted gently, with all its doors wide open, as if it couldn't wait to snap its jaws shut on the people and roar away with them. Susan dashed into the first car to make sure of not being left, only to see Hal walking on outside the cars. What the—? Well—Susan ducked out again and raced after him.

"Why—?"

"Saves time to be up front," he informed her.

As they went forward there were fewer people, and the first car was occupied only by John Kent Haven.

Seeing him, Hal stopped short, but it was too late to turn back. "Hi," he said, passing up John Kent Haven and sitting across the aisle at the far end.

John Kent Haven grunted and looked out the window.

Susan had really hoped Tommy O'Donnell might decide to take one of the tickets and come, but no, out of their whole school here was nobody but skinny old stuck-up John Kent Haven. So it didn't really matter that Mother had made her comb down her hair. Unless she were to meet some Stranger.

A fat man waddled into the car and settled down with his newspaper, and then came a spidery woman wearing clean white gloves. A girl with long hair and glasses. A plump light Negro boy, very neatly dressed.

The train gasped and stopped breathing, as if it had given up hope all at once and died. Then its doors suddenly slid together and it moved matter-of-factly

off along the iron trestle.

Why did they call it a *subway* out here, where it went way up in the air? People looked odd from the top; Susan watched them crawling along the sidewalks and into the shops. Then the train stopped at a crow's nest of a station, and some more people got on.

Further on they collected a little Spanish-looking girl who glanced timidly out of the corners of her eyes, and smoothed her skirt carefully beneath her, like an old lady, before she sat down across from Susan.

The train rumbled on between the dirty upstairs windows of old tenements, between haughty tall units

of new housing developments. Then the street came up and the train went down and they were underground, with ghosts staring in at the windows—their own reflections, looking back at them. Susan's face, solemn and opalescent, hovered on the windowpane between the fat man, who was nothing but knees and a newspaper, and the thin woman, stiff as a plaster dress model except for her fingers in the white gloves that kept mechanically working at her black leather purse.

At 125th two Negro boys got on. They wore old dungarees, the kind Hal might wear to play ball in, but their jackets—Hal would never have worn either of those jackets, anywhere, any time. One had patches all over it—around the armholes, on the elbows, and down the front; and the other was a sleazy kind of artificial black leather.

Underprivileged, thought Susan.

She glanced at her brother, who was gazing at the newcomers over sternly crossed arms. Susan immediately felt sympathetic toward them, especially the short chubby button-nosed one with the patches, who was racing down the aisle.

"C'mon James, let's go up here," he was urging. "Where you sees the track jumping at you, like."

"Yeh, yeh, yeh," said his tall thin companion tolerantly, sauntering after. "Don't get in a sweat, Dobbs

Henry, I'm follering."

Juvenile delinquents, thought Susan.

Heads turned all the way, eyes watchfully following the two young outsiders. They reached the front window and hunched to peer out.

There was a shrieking of iron wheels on iron tracks. The train stopped. The noise hushed so suddenly the world seemed to have stopped. The lights went out.

It seemed as if Susan's thoughts went out too, as the whole world vanished into silence and darkness.

again, strangers

THE EMERGENCY LIGHTS went on, pale and sickly, and Susan found she could breathe again. She peered through the murk at the others, who were peering through the murk back.

"If this isn't the limit!" said the fat man across the aisle. "Third time this year I've got stuck in the subway!"

The train gave a lurch and a gasp, started up, shuddered violently, stopped again. The emergency lights went out, then on again.

The rear door of the car popped open and the conductor hurried in, swinging a flashlight. "Just a power failure," he said briskly. "We'll have it fixed in a jiffy." He opened the front door and jumped with a thud onto the tracks.

Two other thuds followed. Then a roar from the

impatient conductor.

"You brats get back in there!" The boys scrambled back and the conductor's face appeared behind them, ferociously lighted from below by the flashlight.

"You could get electrocuted!" he warned, and disappeared again.

"Eeeee-lectrocuted!" echoed the boy called James, and there was a storm of hiccuppy giggles from his friend.

Some of the passengers crowded down to the front of the train to try to see what was happening.

"I can't see. What's going on?" asked John Kent Haven.

"They brung a bunch of guys in a handcar," reported the round-faced boy. "They got flashlights. Now they standing around talking things over."

"Prob'ly something got on the tracks. The other day up at Mt. Vernon (that's where I live, Mt. Vernon) somebody threw a baby buggy on the train tracks, and the trains couldn't run for two hours." (Whose voice was that? Oh, it must be that neat-looking Negro boy.)

"Baby buggy!" repeated the crackling voice of James Leather-Coat. "Listen at that, Dobbs Henry! Whose baby buggy, Kid? Yours?"

Hoodlums, thought Susan. *The trainload of trapped people were terrorized by two young gangsters.*

"Much less than a baby buggy could do it," went on the unperturbed voice. "Anything that breaks the connection."

"But, two hours!" protested the white-gloved lady. "Why, I'm on my way to see my sister in the hospital; I've got to get there before noon!"

The fat man came blundering back up the aisle, stepped heavily on Susan's foot, and sat down. "I daresay we all have things to do, of more or less importance," he said reprovingly.

"At least, we all think our own things are important," said someone with a laugh in her voice.

"Well, ours really are," said Hal. "We're due at the CBS-TV station at eleven o'clock."

"Really? How funny!" said the laughing voice. "So am I!"

"You mean you-all on TV?" exclaimed Dobbs Henry. "You sing or dance or something?"

"Sing or dance? *Me?*" said Hal.

"You're going to the Science Searchlight program, right?" said the Mt. Vernon boy. "You got tickets for it at school, right? That's me, too."

"If there are workmen out there, why don't they get the track fixed?" fumed the fat man. "What in the world is holding them up?"

"My poor sister will be wondering what could have happened to me," lamented the lady. "It isn't good for her health to worry."

"I sure did want to be at that broadcast," said the Mt. Vernon boy. "Now I wish I'd stayed home, I could at least have seen it. It's going to be about Quasars."

"Whatcha mean, Quasars?" (Dobbs Henry again.)

One of the young hoodlums showed a surprising interest in the rich children's affairs, thought Susan. (Rich? Well, richer than Dobbs Henry.)

"Radio waves," said Hal.

"No, they're not," said John Kent Haven vehemently. "They're quasi-stellar radio sources."

"Whoopee!" jeered the black-coated boy.

The other hoodlum worked off his aggressions by making nasty remarks about everybody, thought Susan.

"That's right, quasi-stellar radio sources," repeated the Mt. Vernon boy approvingly. "Gosh, how do you remember those big words?"

"What I like," said the laughing voice, though more seriously, "is the thought that we'll be able to see something that happened billions of years ago. Imagine! See it happening! Only of course, now we won't."

Susan jerked her head around. Hal never told her it would be anything like that. That would be worthwhile. But could she believe it? The speaker must be that girl with stringy black hair. She must be smart, though.

"If we're all going to the same place, we ought to get acquainted," said the boy from Mt. Vernon. "I'm Terry McIlvane."

"I'm Jennifer Morgenstern, from Yonkers," said the girl with dark hair.

A soft, breathless voice, not heard before, almost whispered, "I'm Cecilia Lopez. I go to that program too."

"We're Hal and Susan Hunter from White Plains, and over there's John Kent Haven. From our same school."

"Well, take a bow, Dobbs Henry, this gotta be our turn," said that intrusive voice from up front. It was maddening, like soap in your eyes. "Tell 'em we from Harlem. Sure 'nuff? Harlem?—Sure 'nuff."

"But we got no tickets to no show," said his friend. "Say, James, I bet them's the tickets Mr. Levy told us about. I thought at the time we shoulda took 'em."

"Yeh—they were free, weren't they?" said the other "Nothin' for nothin'."

"If they can't fix this train," said the fat man, "They should get us out of here. We could go along the catwalk. Seems to me there's very little consideration—"

"Maybe we're blocked by another train," said the lady. "Maybe the exits are shut off. The conductor should come back and inform us, in any case."

"Maybe he'll never come back, Lady," said the one called James. "Maybe we'll never get out. Maybe we is all buried alive in here together! What a comedown!" He laughed.

Nobody else laughed.

That was the tragic day when the subway tunnels of New York finally gave way under the strain, thought Susan. *And whole trainloads of passengers were crushed by the weight of the great city.*

She thought of all the rocks and pavement and buildings. Was it really getting harder to breathe? Was her heart really pounding and her ears beginning to ring?

"Ay, *mi madre*, is it true? Buried alive?" The little Spanish girl had slipped across the aisle for company.

"No, of course not," said Susan in a tone that came out of her tight throat surprisingly calm and confident.

(Why, that was the tone Mother always used to make *her* feel better! Was that all there was to it— did Mother just *say* those things?)

The smoky darkness seemed to seep out of the tunnel and spread over the whole world . . .

And then a bright coin of light flew through the

gloom and leaped into the car; the conductor's voice followed it, and lastly, the conductor himself bounded in, his cap pushed back and a grin on his face.

"All fixed up! Everybody O.K.?"

The lights went on. All the dim silhouettes that had been nothing but human beings in general turned suddenly into flesh and blood people with all sorts of peculiarities. Jennifer had braces on her teeth and thick glasses. The fat man, though so confident in the dark, immediately hid himself in his newspaper again, as though shy, in the light.

James and Dobbs Henry hunched at the front, muttering and snickering. It was hard to believe they had ever been part of the general conversation.

"We're too late for the show," said the boy from Mt. Vernon.

"I wonder if they'll give us tickets for next week," said Hal. "Maybe we could use the same ones." He absently fumbled in his pockets, then looked accusingly at Susan. "Where's your sweater?"

Susan looked around vaguely. Her sweater. When it got hot, she must have taken it off. But where?

"You left it in the bus," said Hal. "Stupid!"

Susan bit her lip. Cecilia could hear. Maybe Jennifer, too.

Jennifer didn't seem to have heard. She said, "Are you going to the broadcast next week?"

"If my teacher will fix it up again about meeting me at the station," said Terry. "So Mother will let me go."

"Same with us," said Hal. "Say, how's about we try to get together, and all go? Under the station clock at quarter to eleven?"

Nobody answered. Nobody could, because the train had let out a terrific bellow and started off. In the uproar they could no longer hear each other, and it was embarrassing to stare, so once again everyone was separate, and the eyes of all looked past each other.

Again, they were all strangers, thought Susan.

no tune

TERRY MCILVANE DECIDED it would be dumb to go straight back home. Now that he was downtown on his own, he should do something exciting. But what? None of the old kid things, Empire State Building, Statue of Liberty, Central Park . . . Why not the Museum? He'd dragged his parents through it several times, and they would go with him again if he insisted, no doubt; but much better to go on his own. What was that new exhibit he'd read about? Some Indian thing. But how would he get there? He might have to ask for help, and he hated to do that.

There was the uptown subway—he could see it across the no-man's land of tracks. There were trains and stairways and tunnels, but where was the street? And once he found the outside world, where was the Museum? He'd always been taken by car, before.

As he hesitated at the top of the steps, he heard someone calling. Since it was his own name, it carried distinctly to his ears through the meaningless clatter of the trains.

"Terry! Wait a minute!"

It was that boy who knew so much about Quasars. (And knew he knew.) What was his name? John Something Something. He was shoving past people like he didn't know they were there—like they were bushes or something.

Terry sidled to the edge of the passage so as not to be trampled. What was the big deal? Like, did Terry have something the other guy wanted, or had the other guy found Terry's billfold or something?

"Could I go with you?" John asked breathlessly when he finally made it. "I don't exactly know the way."

"Well, I'm not going home right now," said Terry, making up his mind about that on the spot. "Why don't you go with those other kids who live in White Plains? There they are now, on the other platform."

"Those jerks?" said John.

Terry decided against him for sure. If you couldn't get along with the people you knew—ordinary, all-right people like Susan and Hal—it was usually your own fault. And if you called them names to strangers, you were really out of it—even if you did know about

Quasars and other science topics.

"Well, anyway, that's the way you get home," said Terry, pointing. "No problem. Just be sure to take a Jerome-Woodlawn train (number 4, I think it is) and you'll get back to wherever you came from." He started to turn away.

"No! You don't understand! I want to go with you!" said John. And while Terry still hesitated, searching for a convincing excuse to be rid of him, John added pleadingly, "I *like* people like you!"

That did it! Terry just threw him one glance and left.

Don't let it get to you, he's just some kind of nut, Terry told himself, but the shaking in his stomach was matched by the shaking in his knees.

A song jumped into his head. "We shall overcome, We shall overcome, We shall overcome some day; Deep in our hearts, We can be sure, We shall overcome some day."

Gradually his faltering legs got back their strength and he could walk briskly again. Or rather, he could do it naturally, without faking. You had to fake if there was no other way, but a tune in your head sure helped.

The Freedom Marchers had learned that, and he had seen the evidence on his parents' home movie films. They moved along in the midst of flying rocks, bottles, rotten fruit, people spitting, and sometimes bullets. Sometimes they were singing out loud, and sometimes the tune must have been only in their heads, but you could tell from the way they walked that they had a tune to keep them going. Once in a while their mouths twisted a little or their eyes turned involuntarily toward the cattle prod or the stream from the fire hose that was blasting at them, but they never flinched or broke the rhythm.

Terry, of course, had never had anything thrown at him, nor walked in a Freedom March, though his mother and father had, when they were younger. He had barely even had anyone call him names. Just that red-headed boy at school who wasn't quite bright, who yelled at him, "Eenie, meenie, minie, mo, Catch a Nigger by the toe," and then had to stay in at recess for a whole week. That was when Terry was seven; and Terry had felt mean about the whole thing, because that kid didn't know what he was doing. He was just trying to get in good with the others by doing out in the open what the others were doing around the corner.

But besides being sorry for the kid, he also felt mad and mean to realize that in some way he, Terry, was even lower than somebody who didn't have good sense.

Terry had gradually made friends with most of the

kids. They came to his home, and he went to theirs. He was the only Negro in the class, since the house his parents had bought with the help of a white friend was not in the Negro section of town. And he got good grades, and the teachers liked him just as the kids did. As long as they were all doing things together, Terry had no problems and forgot for long hours at a time that there was anything different about him.

Then something would happen like John's remark. Somehow, it had taken all the fun out of his plan, and he was about ready to go home. But he didn't want to run into the other kids, in case their train hadn't picked them up yet. So he marched on, as if he knew where he was going, and saw the sign "Telephones"—and did. He would look up the Museum in the phone book, and then he wouldn't have to ask for help.

After looking under "M" for Museum and "N" for Natural History, with no success, he finally remembered that lots of things were listed under "New York, City of"; so he found it: American Museum of Natural History, Central Park West and 79th St.

But he didn't know where Central Park West was, so he was as bad off as before.

He had to ask, so he braced himself and stopped a kindly-looking old man who didn't seem to be going somewhere as fast as the rest.

"Pardon me, but could you please tell me how to get to the American Museum of Natural History?"

The old man stopped and looked him over, a pleased smile spreading across his face. "I really don't know, Son, but I'll help you to find out," he said.

Terry felt doubtful; what he wanted was somebody who knew. But he was in for it now. The old man all but took him by the hand.

He beckoned to a uniformed official who was hurrying by. "Can you tell us how to find the American Museum of Natural History?"

"Cripe, I don't exactly know," said the official. He peered around, then gave a low whistle. Another official halfway down the corridor turned and came back. The first official put the same question to the second official. Terry almost laughed; he was like the boy with the golden goose, picking up a whole parade of followers.

But fortunately, this official was the kind who knew everything, and he gave Terry splendid instructions, and the small crowd of advisers began to disperse, as Terry thanked them all.

The old man was the last to turn away, and after he had gone a step or two, he turned back and shook Terry's hand again.

"If only all colored people were as nice and polite

as you, they would have no trouble at all!" he said.

Terry couldn't answer, but it didn't matter. The old man was so misted over with his own kind thoughts that he didn't notice the lack of response.

Terry went on, trying to remember the directions he had received.

Why should such a little thing as the old man's remark make him feel so ugly? It was just that it came so soon after John's—both proving what Terry always tried to forget, that he was different.

Maybe he should go live in Harlem. But he'd be different there, too.

"Take the shuttle to Times Square . . ." That wasn't so difficult. "Get the Seventh Avenue Uptown Local . . ." He had to hunt for that. "Get off at Fifty-ninth and wait for the IND Eighth Avenue . . ." Or was it Sixth Avenue?

"How do you get to the Natural History Museum?" Terry asked the man in the refreshment booth.

"Take the next train to the second stop, and you're there," said the man. "How about a candy apple or a pretzel?"

"I'll take a butterscotch," said Terry, spinning a quarter over the counter. He enjoyed the chewy butterscotch and watching the odd people. The train came pretty soon, and sure enough, he got off at the second stop and walked straight into the museum.

There were the old dusty Diplodocus and his friends; and the fierce bears and tigers in their tight, bright little jungles around the wall; and finally he found the Plains and Woodland Indians.

The exhibit was newer than the others, but arranged somewhat the same. More stuff than you could understand in a month. But Terry was drawn to the miniature scenes—houses, ceremonials, life episodes, which were so delicately made and well-proportioned that he seemed to shrink until he was part of this strange, different, world.

After a while he got tired of it and went into the new Minerals exhibit. He could have stayed there for hours, but the thought kept pricking him that he'd better get home soon, or the parents wouldn't let him come next week.

At dinner that night, his father asked, "Well, how was your excursion?" and proceeded with great concentration to slice the roast.

This gave Terry time to debate with himself whether perhaps he should pretend that everything had gone off as planned. It would save a lot of fuss. It would be fun to try to build up a convincing account of the broadcast he hadn't seen.

But he didn't know that much about Quasars, and

Dad probably did. And besides, the real story was too interesting to keep. So he told it. (Except about John Kent Haven and the old man.)

"You mean you had to sit in the train without lights or anything, not knowing what might happen?" his mother gasped, laying her palm along her smooth cheek as she always did when she was disturbed, her rings sparkling, and her large soft eyes widening. "How long did it last? And those rowdy slum boys you describe—why, they might have gone berserk and knifed you or something!"

Terry met his father's eye with an answering glint of manly amusement.

"Oh, I guess it wasn't that much of a crisis, Mother," he said. "It was over in half an hour."

"Man, I bet it was great!" said his little brother Lennie, impressed at last. "Too bad it got over so soon."

"Actually, rather an interesting experience, eh?" said Dad.

"Yeah, Dad, it really was," Terry responded eagerly. "You know—meeting up by accident, and then getting so well acquainted. We talked about going to the broadcast again next week, and meeting downtown. Don't you think that would be all right? I could go, couldn't I?"

"We-ell, don't count on them," said Dad. "Spur-

of-the-moment acquaintances can prove pretty dis-
appointing."

"Yeah," Terry agreed reluctantly. Like that nut,
John, and the nice old man.

The phone rang, a welcome interruption to his
thoughts. When he answered it, he was hardly surprised to hear a stranger's voice, one that he recognized.

"Hello. Terry McIlvane?"

"Yeah. Speaking," said Terry.

"I'm Hal Hunter. You know, the guy you met on
the subway today?"

"Yeah, sure, Hal, I recognized your voice."

"Good! Well, Terry, I was just wondering. You
know, we're having a kind of skating party Friday
night, with eats here afterward, and we were just
wondering, maybe you could come too. My dad
would take you home."

Terry didn't speak right away. Something stopped
his throat. Hal liked him.

He started to say, "Sure! I'd like that."

But he had waited a while to speak, so his voice
would sound straight, and Hal spoke again just as he
did. Hal's voice sounded a little different this time.

Hal said, "I hope you don't think I'm being fresh.
I know you don't really know me, but my Dad's a
lawyer, same as your dad is, and he recognized your

name right away. That is—your father *is* Terence
McIlvane, the Civil Rights lawyer?"

So that was it.

"Yeah. Yeah, that's my dad. Well, it's real nice of
you, and I'd like to, but Friday, well, I got something
else I got to do."

Terry hung up and went back to the table. He
walked as jauntily as he could, so the family wouldn't
ask him what the matter was; but somehow, there
wasn't any tune.

the lasso

AT DINNER HAL had told his parents the story of the Great Train Hold-Up—or tried to tell it, Susan interrupting every other sentence.

"And when this girl said she was going to a TV broadcast, one of the hoods asked, 'You on TV?'—as if she could have been."

"Who knows?" said Susan. "You get all ages of performers these days. Look at the Four Corners—that Southeast Corner is only fifteen. Besides, that girl looked something like a folk singer, that long hair and those funny glasses."

"Those glasses were for near-sightedness; they're like the wrong end of binoculars, that's why her eyes looked so far away."

"Just the same, it was cool, like her eyes were fishes swimming around. I think they should make a fad of glasses like that," said Susan.

Hal tried to ignore this annoyance. "And then this girl said, 'How many of you are going to the TV broadcast,' and we all said, 'I am,' and—"

"It wasn't Jennifer, it was Terry who said that, and don't you remember, earlier, how it just happened to come up because of that lady who was yelling about her dumb appointment? If she hadn't said that, we never would have known we were all going, and it never would have happened!"

"And so what?" retorted Hal. "Anyway, we got to talking about Quasars—"

"And you should have heard John Kent Haven showing off how much he knew!"

"And then they fixed the train."

"Oh, but they didn't get it fixed until after the worst moment of all, when that delinquent said we were going to be buried alive. And I was petrified, but I had to try to comfort Cecilia, because she was more scared than I was. You leave out all the most interesting parts," said Susan.

The parents smiled, and Susan complacently cut her bread in strips, the way he hated.

"Well, all right, here's something *you* left out— about losing your sweater."

He was sorry the moment he'd said it. Susan's carelessness immediately leaped into the center of the

stage, like a glum triumphant ghost.

"Not your lovely sweater from Grandma!" said Mother—and bit her lip.

"I'm just thankful your head's screwed on," said Daddy, trying to laugh it away. "Such a nice little head, I'd hate you to lose *that*."

It was too late. Susan was hanging her hair down in her potatoes.

"How about another piece of chicken, Chick?" asked Daddy.

"No thank you, I'm not hungry," said Susan.

"Can you come home from school early Monday so we can look for a new dress for Mary Kay's party?" asked Mother.

"I don't think I'll go to the party," said Susan.

(His parents didn't seem to know how to handle her at all.)

"Which of those kids today did you like best?" he asked.

Susan shrugged and mumbled, "I d'know, they were all a bunch of creeps."

"That Jennifer was kinda nice," said Hal.

"I liked the little Spanish one better—she was cute," said Susan.

"But the one who was really swell was that Negro boy from Mt. Vernon—what was his name?" (Hal remembered perfectly.)

"Terry McIlvane," said Susan, coming to life like a wilted flower stuck in water. "Yeah, he was nice."

"Terry McIlvane," muttered Dad. "Now why does that name ring a bell? Oh, I know. Terence McIlvane is the lawyer who won all those Civil Rights cases. You say this was a Negro boy from Mt. Vernon? Must be the same family."

"That figures," said Hal, and Susan, now fully restored, said, "Of course it is. You could tell from how he acted that he *was* somebody."

"Why don't you invite this boy over for a visit?" suggested Daddy.

Hal put down his chicken leg. That was a strange idea. He could hardly visualize walking down their street with Terry. Only white boys ever played on his street. Even though there were quite a few Negroes in his school now, a few in his classes and lots in Gym, they always went right home every afternoon to their own neighborhoods.

"That would be a very nice thing to do," said Mother.

"He wouldn't come," said Susan.

"It was just an idea," said Daddy.

Hal ate his pie. He hated to do anything as odd as this, but after all, Terry wasn't just a Negro kid at school, he was something special.

"I'll call him up and ask him," said Hal.

He got a little panicked while the phone was ring-
ing against his ear, wondering what he would say. But
as soon as he heard Terry's nice calm voice he was
glad, and thought how pleased Terry was going to be
to get the invitation.

Then Terry turned him down.

Hal went back to the table, where the family
looked at him expectantly. "I don't understand it.
What did I say?" Hal mumbled.

"What do you mean, what did you say?" asked
Susan. "You invited him over. What did *he* say?"

"He said he couldn't come. That he had something
else to do."

"I told you so," said Susan.

"Maybe he did have something else to do," said
Dad, opening his newspaper.

"But you never finished the story," said Mother.
"What about the 'hoods' as you call them? Did they
show any interest in your plan?"

"Oh, no, Mother," said Susan. "They just got lost
as soon as the lights went on and things got back to
normal. They were real gangsters, you know, and if
they'd had a chance they'd probably have mugged us.
You can't imagine how different they were from
Terry; even if they were all Negroes. He was wonderful, just like us."

"Wonderful—just like us!" mimicked Hal. "Mugging! You don't even know what mugging is!"

But making fun of Susan didn't take away the sting of being turned down by Terry. What was *with* this guy? Still nursing his grievance on Monday, Hal looked more critically at Franklin, the Negro boy in his Science class, with whom he also played volley-ball. But there wasn't much to see. Franklin was quiet in class, where there were few Negroes, and noisy in gym, where there were few white boys. He certainly wasn't at all interested in Hal, and that must be how Terry had felt, too.

Hal explained to Mr. Whitman, the Science teacher, about their experience on Saturday, and Mr. Whitman promised to get them more tickets. He handed them out the next day, and as Hal took his, he suddenly wondered if Mr. Levy, Dobbs Henry's teacher, were handing them out again, too.

"*Mr. Levy told us about them tickets,*" Dobbs Henry had said. "*I thought at the time we shoulda took some.*"

He had sounded like he really wished he were go-ing.

Why didn't I say on the subway, 'Hey, why don't you come too?' Hal thought to himself. I bet Dobbs Henry might have done it. He really wanted to, but that real hood, James, wouldn't let him.

Hal remembered Dobbs Henry's lively, curious

face. I bet if I'd asked him, he wouldn't have turned me down, he thought.

Just for kicks, he looked up "Dobbs Henry" in the Manhattan phone directory. It was such an unusual name he thought he would spot it right away. But it wasn't there. Then he realized that James had said "Dobbs-Henry" as if it were a double name. And even if it wasn't, your father didn't always have the same name as you. And then, too, Hal realized suddently that some people didn't even have phones.

In Harlem, maybe hardly anyone did. Hal had never been in Harlem. Nobody he knew had ever been in Harlem. Of course, famous athletes, and musicians—and maids—often came from there.

It really would be interesting to know somebody who actually lived there. But how? The more difficult it seemed, the more Hal wished it could happen.

Finally he figured out a way. Mr. Levy was a Science teacher, and so was Mr. Whitman.

"Do you know a teacher in Harlem named Mr. Levy who teaches Science?" he asked, stopping at the desk after school.

"Do you have any idea how many teachers there are in the New York area who teach Science, for one reason or another?" asked Mr. Whitman. "I don't at the moment bring to mind a Mr. Levy. Why?"

Hal looked at Mr. Whitman's amused face dubiously.

"Well, there was a guy in the subway last week when we got stuck who said he had a Science teacher by that name. He was from Harlem."

"Well, I might search it out in some of my archives —teacher's directory or something," said Mr. Whitman. "Do you have a good reason?"

"I want his phone number," said Hal, ignoring Mr. Whitman's ill-timed humor.

Next day Mr. Whitman called him to the desk. "Stephen Levy, P.S. 39, and here's the phone number. But what's it all about?"

Hal muttered, "Well, it was that kid. He really wanted to come, but I thought he needed some—you know, encouragement."

Mr. Whitman was silent. Hal had thought he would be. Teachers and parents don't really like kids' ideas, as a rule.

"What's wrong with that?" Hal burst out.

"Nothing; except—don't you think it's a little like trying a lasso him, as if he were a calf?"

Hal's gaze jumped to meet Mr. Whitman's blue eyes. This time, Mr. Whitman wasn't kidding.

"Why don't you think about somebody nearer to home?" Mr. Whitman said bluntly. "Why do you think Franklin didn't take a ticket for the show? He's every bit as good a student as you are, you know."

Franklin? What did he have to do with it?

"Did you ever ask him to ride down on the subway

with you? Did you ever think Franklin might need some encouragement?"

"Well, no," said Hal.

"There's one ticket left. I bet he'd go if you suggested it."

"Well, O.K.," said Hal discontentedly. He dropped the slip with Mr. Levy's telephone number into the wastebasket.

This was what always happened when you really wanted to do something. Grown-ups got hold of it and turned it into something you didn't have in mind at all.

Talk about lassos!

people like you

JOHN KENT HAVEN TRAILED Terry McIlvane along the crowded platform. He hoped Terry would look around and see him and say, "Hey, you're the boy who knows about Quasars. Why don't you come with me?"

But Terry never looked back. He walked as if the ground simply disappeared after he'd walked on it, and all that mattered still lay ahead.

John Kent Haven wanted to run after Terry; he wanted to shout, "I know lots of other things you'd be interested in! Just wait, and I'll tell you!"

Of course, he couldn't say all that. Anyway, his feet were weighted with lead and his tongue was stiff as a board, like in a nightmare.

Finally he managed to call out in a creaky voice, "Terry, wait for me a minute! Please!"

Terry heard him through all the hubbub and turned to see who had called.

John waved and struggled after him through the masses of bodies, all apparently trying to get in his way.

"Could I go with you?" John asked breathlessly. And then, because Terry just looked at him, he added in what, to his horror, came out as a sort of whine, "I don't exactly know the way."

"I'm not going home now," said Terry. "Look, why don't you go with them?" And he pointed out Susan and Hal, boarding the other train.

How could John tell Terry that Susan and Hal didn't want him? He said something or other, while the conviction grew on him that Terry didn't want him either. Either Terry thought John was queer and unattractive, with his high shoulders and thin face and big words; or he thought John wouldn't like him, Terry, because he was a Negro.

Well, John could eliminate the latter notion, anyway.

"I—I like people like you!" he stammered.

Terry's happy-shaped face froze into a tight mask; Terry turned and went. John was left staring after him, while embarrassment swarmed hotly up his body, settling in splotches on his neck and forehead.

Inertly, John let himself be shoved and jostled

along. One thing he would not do, was go scampering
after Hal and Susan.

The current swirled him up a stairway, through a
corridor, down an arcade. He was out on the street,
he was walking down the sidewalk, and still he could
think of nothing but the calamity with Terry. *People
like you, people like you, people like you.*

Terry had heard the part which meant, "I won't
hold it against you that you're a Negro," and hadn't
heard the other part: "You're a guy who might be
interested in the stars and the stones and all the great
discoveries there are to make! You're a guy I'd like
for a friend!"

Oh well, it was just the kind of dumb thing he was
always doing. I'm just a nut, John thought. He was
sure of this at least half the time. The other half,
though, when he was not thinking about himself, he
was happy—because of the sky, the earth, the sea; the
way Math always worked out true to itself, and the
surprises in words.

His mother guessed at these feelings, but she knew
that he needed someone other than herself to share
them with.

"Sometime you'll meet people who are interested
in what you're interested in," she told him, "And
you'll have lots of wonderful friends."

That was why she wanted him to get the scholar-

ship, so he could go to the private school. She was a
widow, earning their living, and she couldn't afford
to pay for the private school; but she said he would
get along better there. She said he would find his kind
of people.

But what if he didn't get the scholarship? The
grades were easy. But being an "all-round boy" was
for John not only hard, it was impossible.

John realized that he'd walked quite a distance from
the station. Where in the heck was he going?

("The Havens," his mother often lamented,
"haven't a practical bone in their bodies. Your father,
a brilliant man, could get lost in his own back yard.")

John wasn't surprised to be lost.

Like the others, he was walking along as fast as
possible, but the others, he assumed, knew where they
were going. He'd have to ask somebody.

A couple of boys in private school blazers marched
along in front of him, barking short remarks to each
other like actors who knew not only their cues, but
how the whole play was going to come out. (And
John wasn't in it.)

A group of girls passed by, chattering and giggling.
They had no script to follow, and would stop for anything—even John—but he wouldn't know how to talk
to them, nor trust their answers, anyway.

A woman in a crimson sari with a gilt dot on her

forehead met and engulfed him in delicate perfume and swept on, giving him a momentary vision of Indian temples and elephants; and two men walked behind him for some distance, vehemently talking in French. He forgot everything else for a while, trying to understand what they were saying, but could get only about one word in twenty, though his mother had taught him a little French.

He looked searchingly at the women. He was rather inclined to trust mothers. But some of them were worrying along with their children, and others were all wound up inside with their thoughts and their plans, glancing in the shop windows and figuring busily. He couldn't bring himself to break in on them.

Random boys threaded through the crowd, yelling to each other over their shoulders, too energetic to bide by the general pace. Some were wide-awake and vigorous-looking. John would have liked to pitch a question to one of them, but he couldn't get it off fast enough.

Without warning, he plunged into a dark wooden tunnel, a dusty shield for a noisy bulldozing construction job. When he came out, he was more hopelessly lost than ever, in a forest of shining sharp-cornered towers that bounced the sunshine back and forth like a huge game of mirrors.

Desperately he put out a hand to the next person

he met, a neat, efficient-looking businessman.

"Don't bother me, please, I'm in a hurry," said the person, pushing past him.

John backed up against a shop window, glancing unseeingly at its wonderful display of leather goods. The world went right on past. He was like a leaf lodged at the edge of a river; the moment he moved he would be whirled helplessly along again. Would this go on till night came, bringing some dark street, with a steel arm across his throat?

"Hey, fella!"

Was somebody actually talking to him? John looked around incredulously, and had a new shock. A sailor was hailing him, a big sunburned guy with very blue eyes and a wide grin and curly red hair under his cuffed white hat.

John had seen many movies about sailors on the town who relieved their pent-up energy by indulging in crude, practical jokes on everyone in their way.

He looked around wildly for a possible escape, but he was hemmed in. The sailor neatly cleft a path through the crowd, and pulled up beside John. He was huge.

"You look kinda lost," he said. "Where you bound for?"

"Grand Central Station," said John weakly.

The sailor smiled. "By the strangest coincidence,

me too," he said. "After me, son."

He started off, and John, willy nilly, went after him, feeling as if he were being sucked along by a powerful force, thinking vaguely about gravitational fields and wondering what new and dangerous orbit he was being drawn into.

He was so dazed and apprehensive that it was quite a surprise to him to look up and see the massive sculpture on the top of the Grand Central Station, and to realize that the sailor, now yards ahead of him, was cupping his hands to yell, "O.K., now?" and disappearing forever without doing him the slightest harm.

Sailors, he thought, are all kinds of people.

The clock in the Grand Concourse said 12:30. This was the exact time his mother had figured he would be through, and call her, so she could start off to fetch him at the end of the subway. He found the phone booth.

"How was the program?" she asked.

"I'll tell you all about it," John promised. He grinned to himself: she'd have a fit!

Everything seemed easy now. John merely drifted along till he saw the subway sign and followed the arrows to the train. He got on, sat down and remained in a comfortable haze of weariness until the train came up from underground, when he suddenly noticed something was wrong. Everything was strange; it was like a nightmare, or Alice in Wonderland—he'd gone into one tunnel and come out another!

Of course! He'd got on the wrong train, in spite of his mother and Terry both warning him he must take the Jerome-Woodlawn. This was the Dyre Avenue, which went, who knew where? So now he was being hurtled along as fast as possible in the wrong direction. Nobody looked at him, nobody cared. Who would rescue him this time?

Answer, obviously: himself. He just had to get off and go back.

So he did. He got off at the next stop, went down the steps, crossed the street, went up again—and came face to face with the same grinning chewing-gum ad. He went down and crossed the other street, and the ad was across the tracks; he'd found his way.

A worried-looking lady touched his arm.

"Excuse me," she said, "But is this the uptown or the downtown platform?"

"Downtown," said John politely. "If you want uptown, go down the steps and cross the street that way."

"Thanks ever so much," she said, adding apologetically, "I'm always getting lost. Seems like you young folks always know the way."

if i had a brother

CECILIA MOVED TIMIDLY along the train platform, wishing she were not alone, wishing she had a brother like that blonde girl, Susan.

If she had a brother, he would be with her now and she wouldn't feel scared.

If she had a brother, Papa would let her go many more places and do many more things—and she would want to, if she had a brother.

The blonde girl and *her* brother passed Cecilia. The girl looked around and smiled back at her. She even paused as if she wanted to talk, but Cecilia dropped her eyes quickly. Even though Cecilia was pleased to be smiled at, she thought the girl (Susan) was a little unmannerly to stare about and wave at somebody who was practically a stranger. She did look very nice. She was very large, of course, and her hair was not well-kept.

"And if I had a brother," Cecilia thought, "he would be quite different from that one. The way that one hurries off without waiting for her or even looking back to see if she's coming! The way he acts so superior! The way he was so mean about her sweater! My brother would see that I walked ahead of him, and he would help me if I needed it, and even though he would realize that he was stronger and wiser than I, he would never make me feel unhappy about it."

But now Cecilia had to stop admiring her imaginary brother and start worrying about what to do. She had to find her way back home, which she had never expected to have to do. The only reason Papa had let her go in the first place was because he himself could walk her to the subway, and her teacher had promised to see her to the right train on her way home.

So, Cecilia knew exactly how to get to the big clock in the waiting room where Miss Purcell had agreed to meet her. But Miss Purcell would have gone long since, and Cecilia really had no idea how to get home again.

She looked for signs. Over the stairway was a sign that said "Grand Central Station, New York Central and New Haven Railroads." That was where she would have gone. But now, where should she go?

Her troubles were just beginning. A current of

people carried her through the turnstile and out into a corridor which was large and full and had no signs at all.

Cecilia walked and walked and walked. She sometimes saw a sign that said "Subway," and when she did, she almost ran toward it, as if the subway would disappear if she didn't hurry. But it disappeared anyway, and she found herself walking straight into a blank wall, or heading into a tunnel that announced only too gladly that it was leading somewhere else entirely, "To Street," or "To Taxis," or "To Pan-American Building."

She saw now that she should have stayed down in the subway tunnel, where all the trains came and went. She thought of asking directions from one of the men in uniform who were dashing about here and there. But though her knowledge of English was large enough at ordinary times, and she was often called on to interpret for the neighbors as well as for her parents, the minute she got nervous the words seemed to vanish away. And on the other hand, when she was interpreting, sometimes the English got the upper hand and she would stutter over the Spanish that she had used since she was a baby.

Nevertheless, she was pretty good at both languages, better than her parents. Papa had taken the English course given by the Department of Welfare three times, without ever learning a thing; and so, of course, he couldn't get a job, since he was too small and elderly to do heavy work. When Mama was asked why she didn't try to learn English, since she was so much younger than Papa and should find it easier, she only giggled and twirled her wrist at Papa, as if to say, "If *he* can't do it—it's impossible!"

Cecilia was just about to get up her courage to ask one of the uniformed men for directions when, turning hopelessly into a passage she had gone through before, she suddenly saw straight ahead of her some steps surmounted by the words "IRT Lexington Avenue Uptown."

When she was finally seated on the right train with the right number, Cecilia relaxed for a few moments.

She was tired and hungry, but now it was pleasant to be, because she could picture getting home and resting and telling her story for all the admiring and horrified and awed ears. Dolores and Dominga would be astonished, and Mama would gasp and cry out, and Papa would gravely shake his head, and, alas, decide to take even better care of her from now on. And they would give her all the best food.

But now she began to worry about walking home from the subway. It was not far to walk—maybe eight blocks, and short ones. But it was full of dangers.

The first few blocks were not bad, up the hill past

restaurants, fruit stands, and bakeries with richly packed windows. Then across the magnificent breadth of the Grand Concourse, past the park and the Court House. Another block or two, and over the smoky bridge from which you looked down on a maze of tracks and trains, and past the grim fortress of the Welfare Building.

But then it began to get dreadful. No matter whether she walked on 161st St., where there was such heavy traffic, so that she could hardly get across the street alive and was continually jostled on the sidewalk, or cut across the little old Melrose Park with its splintery wooden shop fronts, or tried any of

the other tenement-lined streets, there would be people. Rough, dirty people, white or colored, child or adult; every one of them frightened her. If she looked at them they might think she was encouraging them to speak; and if she didn't look at them, they might follow her.

With such people, Papa had explained, you didn't know what to expect; all you knew was that they had no rules and no manners, like the Spanish, that you could understand and trust. And the saddest thing of all was that not even all Puerto Ricans could be trusted; some of them were almost as bad as anyone else.

Cecilia had heard Papa say this all her life, but she had never quite believed it, or perhaps rather, never known just what he meant, until that day when she saw the cat. It was a dead cat, and had been thrown under the subway viaduct; but Cecilia couldn't help seeing that it had been tortured. Then she knew what some people must be like.

At last she reached Webster Avenue. She hated Webster Avenue, but up at the end of the block was the place that was not really on Webster Avenue, nor even in New York, but was home.

Cecilia dipped her chin and walked as fast as she could without running.

Some of the people around here knew her, but that wasn't any help.

"Duck-walk! Duck-walk!" somebody shouted, and she knew without looking it was one of those terrible grinning Figueroa boys that lived upstairs.

She passed the milk warehouse, the bar, the grocery store, and the pool hall. A ball came hurtling past her, and somebody laughed; she didn't know for sure whether they'd thrown it at her on purpose.

At last, her own building. But the terror was not yet over. The five-story apartment house was built around a court, which might have been very pleasant long ago when it was filled with grass and trees. Now it was a dark emptiness, where people threw bottles and cans and garbage, and where danger might hide.

Cecilia rushed through it and into the hall. Even the hall was foreign territory, lined with doors from which somebody could dart forth upon her. Up the stairs to the second floor—safety in sight! Even the door was different, with a picture of the Sacred Heart, and the words underneath in Spanish: "God Guards this Home."

Cecilia rat-tat-tatted at the door, the same way her heart was rat-tat-tatting in her chest with relief and happiness.

From inside the expected: *"Qui es?"*

"Me! Cecilia!" she almost sang.

The police lock (a heavy iron brace on the inside of the door) was withdrawn with a rattle. The door opened. Dolores stood there, staring with wide frightened eyes.

Why would she be frightened? Cecilia's heart beat harder than ever and she pushed quite rudely past her sister into the living room.

Dominga, the baby, was sitting stiffly upright on the sofa.

Mama was huddled in the chair.

Where was Papa?

"Papa—?" she turned to Dolores.

"He got run over! On the way back from taking you to the subway," whimpered Dolores. "He's in the hospital. The priest is there. He might—"

Papa! Papa who took care of everything, without whom they could never manage. Small and helpless-looking, yet great and kind Papa.

Through Cecilia's stunned mind came only the usual thought, "If I only had a brother."

the view from
the bridge

THE SUBWAY WAS JAMMED by the time the train
reached Grand Central, and before the departing people had managed to get out, others were struggling to
get in.

Dobbs Henry craned his neck to watch the kids
leave—the handful of people he knew. They soon disappeared.

Or did he know them? Not one of them looked
back. Each was busy trying to find his own way
through the jostling crowd.

Of course he didn't know them. Yet, for a few
minutes he had.

He turned back to James. "Where we going now,
Man?"

James was looking through the crowd into his own
thoughts. His heavy lids were half shut, and his mouth

closed tight. He didn't seem to hear; didn't want to hear. Dobbs Henry had to wait.

At Brooklyn Bridge stop, James suddenly got up and left the train. Dobbs Henry trotted after. James went through the swinging gate so fast it nearly slammed Dobbs Henry in the face. He turned up a corridor, following an arrow pointing to the bridge.

They climbed some steps and came out on the boardwalk that crossed the bridge. Dobbs Henry had never been there before.

The city was behind them. The river ran under them out into the bay, toward the Statue of Liberty and the sea. Overhead loomed the double-arched tower of the bridge from which the skein of supporting cables swept down on each side. They were vast, raking great curved lines from sky to bridge.

"Turn around," said James.

Dobbs Henry looked over his shoulder and froze. Gosh, man!

The skyscrapers of lower Manhattan clustered in one mass of thin spires behind the cables like some dragonfly caught in a spider web.

"Gosh," said Dobbs Henry. "Gosh, it look great. How come you know? You been here before?"

"I been everywhere," said James. "This just one of the places I go."

"It look like somebody make it all, all at once; like

somebody say, 'be there', and it were."

"Millions of cats make that city," said James. "And they don't even know what they doing."

The sight struck a note from a tight string in Dobbs Henry's memory. "Seems kinda like that from Central Park—you looks over the grass and trees at them other tall buildings, like Empire State."

"Oh, yeah," said James, "Where your Dad took you that time."

Dobbs Henry was silent. James mocked about Daddy.

"Where is the old man, anyway?" James asked.

"I dunno," said Dobbs Henry.

"Ain't in jail any more, is he?"

"No." The Welfare Department had put Dobbs Henry's father in jail a while back because he couldn't get work. They thought he wasn't trying hard enough. "Went off to Jersey and got him a job."

He wouldn't add about his mother not hearing for several months. He changed the subject. "Who built this here bridge, anyway?"

James waved toward the bronze plate on the bridge tower. "Whole bunch of guys. Everybody and his uncle got in on the graft."

Well, James knew about such things. He knew all the places and how to get there—wharves, subways, parks. He knew about the gangsters and pushers. He knew Harlem inside out; his older brother was a member of Captains Courageous, one of the strongest gangs. James would be a Captain when he was old enough—if he wasn't a member already. You never knew about James.

"Does we go over to the other side?" asked Dobbs Henry, looking past the second bridge tower to the mass of Brooklyn beyond.

"No, ain't no use in that. Brooklyn just the same as Manhattan, once you gets there. Only from a distance it looks good, like now. Up close, it just another dirty old slummy place."

Dobbs Henry stared from the mounded buildings of Brooklyn to the soaring towers of Manhattan, to the flashing sunlight off the bay, and the moving ships, and the Statue of Liberty. They looked so exciting, so promising. The promise wasn't exactly being made to him—how could it be? But it was to somebody. It couldn't be true that everything, for everybody, was dirt-mean and ugly when you got up close.

"Hey, I wonder did them kids on the subway ever see this?" he suddenly asked.

"Not a chance," said James, with a down-sweep of his hand as if he were swatting flies. "You think them kids would walk over a bridge when they can ride? And they can ride. Every one of them got cars, except maybe the little Spic. And which one you think got the best car of any? That dressed-up colored kid from Mt. Vernon."

"Anyway," Dobbs Henry burst out with sudden, foolhardy defiance, "I wisht we had took them tickets. And Mr. Levy's O.K. I don't know what call you got to hate him. Maybe he caught Timmie stealing, but then he were gonna fix things up for Timmie, too."

James said nothing. This was one topic he never discussed.

They went silently down into the tunnel. Automatically they dodged through the swinging gate without paying. They were just going home. No more excitement today. Dobbs Henry felt fallen apart.

"We going to eat at your place or mine?" Dobbs Henry asked as they got off the subway.

"Yours the closest," said James. It wasn't true. They were just passing James's place—that is, the place where his grown-up sister lived, where he generally stayed.

James's grown-up sister didn't like to feed even James. She had never fed Dobbs Henry; whereas Dobbs Henry's mother always fed them both, and said nothing about it, even though James's portion just came out of somebody else's, since what they had to eat was strictly limited by the Welfare Budget. Enough (enough?) for a mother and three kids, not four. No stretch in that budget.

As they turned the corner of Dobbs Henry's block, James said, "Hey, Man, ain't that your stuff out on the sidewalk?"

Halfway down the block a crowd was gathering. Women leaned on their elbows to look out upper-story windows; kids ran down the sidewalk; men stared and gossiped as they lounged on nearby stoops.

A procession was going up and down the front steps at Dobbs Henry's tenement building. The super, and his brother, and Dobbs Henry's mother: up the steps empty-handed, down the steps loaded, with a chair, a table, the old washing-machine, an armful of pans.

"Man, you're evicted!" James gave Dobbs Henry a slap on the back, as if he were congratulating him.

Dobbs Henry ignored it and sank down on his heels. It was because he was so hungry he felt weak, and besides, it was the first time they'd been evicted.

"Rotten old Welfare," he muttered. "They don't never get around to a thing." The investigator had seen the eviction notice days ago. Mama wasted dimes calling her, and the investigator just whined, "I haven't had time."

"Guess your Daddy didn't send in his check this month," said James. Sneering again when he talked

about Daddy. Didn't have one of his own that was why.

"Guess that job run out. Went somewheres to look for another," Dobbs Henry mumbled.

"Let's go see what your Mama's fixing to do," said James.

"Hi, Henry, James," said Mother, coming out with a basket of dishes and setting them down beside the other things. She looked calm in spite of everything. She wore her old khaki shirt and print skirt and canvas sneakers with as much assurance as if she were dressed for church. "Crackers and peanut butter on the windowsill up in the room."

Dobbs Henry and James ran up the shaky stairs and ate the crackers and cleaned out the peanut butter jar. But this time the place was empty; in the quiet, a rat peeked out of the hole by the stove where he and his kin had shoved aside all the tin can patches Mama nailed on.

James threw the peanut butter jar at the rat. " 'At a baby, duck! But don't worry none. New folks'll be coming, in no time at all, and they'll give you a living! You the guy that never has to worry. You the guy it all made for."

They went downstairs.

"What's going to happen to all our stuff?" Dobbs Henry asked his mother. "What's going to happen to us now?"

His twin sisters were dancing over the heap of furniture as if it were a jungle gym. They were dressed in their best white jumpers and they looked almost as if they were going to a party.

"I'm going to Jeannie's," said Sophronia, the thin one.

"I'm going to Aunt Mary's," said Appolonia, the fat one.

Dobbs Henry still looked at his mother.

"Aunt Mary won't have you," said she. "Because of what you did to Robert last time. Guess you'll have to bunk with James. He's stayed with you often enough."

"O.K.," said Dobbs Henry, not daring to wait for James to say yes or no. He started back toward James's sister's place. James caught his arm.

"All right," he said, "but we won't go over there till after dark."

They waited around the candy store where the Captains Courageous hung out, and James's brother went past them without speaking, which wasn't usual with him.

"Hey, Tim!" James called after him, in a voice unlike his usual bark.

"Get lost, Kid," Tim said over his shoulder, but he spun a quarter through the air to them. They bought chips and a candy bar.

Then they climbed the stairs in James's tenement, and James listened at his sister's door. Something loud was going on. James jerked his head and led Dobbs Henry up to the roof. It was not very cold, and they lay down back to back behind the smokestack.

But some time later in the night, Dobbs Henry got stiff and achy and woke up. James was not there.

trapped

JAMES GOT UP as soon as he was sure Dobbs Henry was asleep. He moved carefully, and though Dobbs Henry flopped over on his back, he didn't wake up.

Dobbs Henry looked young, lying like that with his face turned up, his mouth half open, and his arms flung out. James hoped no junkies would come up on the roof for their fix and take a notion to rough up Dobbs Henry. But they probably wouldn't; junkies weren't dangerous, if you didn't have money.

Besides, Dobbs Henry was all right wherever he was. He was the type that good guys looked after and bad guys weren't likely to bother with.

James went down the stairs and paused on the third floor, looking at the light under Naomi's door. It was quiet in there now. If she was feeling good, she might like to feed him and tell him her troubles.

"Hi, there, Baby Brother," she might say. "How's things? Want some grub?"

But it was so quiet, she might be asleep. Or she might have company. If he went busting in on her—

He went on.

He could go to Aunt Tony Bender's. That was where he'd always lived till about a year ago, and where he was supposed to be living now, only he just couldn't take it any longer. Aunt Tony Bender liked her own kids best, and she couldn't get enough of telling him how bad he was, and how nice the family had been before he came along and killed his mother—did he *ask* to get born?

No, the only place he wanted to live was with Timmie. And Timmie said sure, he could come, right soon now. Just as soon as Timmie got things settled.

Well, James was tired of waiting.

James looked in at the pizza parlor. Tim wasn't there. He tried the hardware store with the pool table in the back; only a couple of dreary old men shooting pool.

The laundromat was closed already. Sometimes the guys hung in there for a while, especially when it was cold outdoors.

The guys stayed in one corner of the steamy, soapy-smelling room, shooting craps and talking, while the mothers in the other end threw their dirty clothes in the tubs and sat around gossiping while they waited. Their kids chased around and hid behind the machines and threw soap at each other. The mothers yelled, "Stop that now! You watch out or I'll take the hide right offen your back!"

The kids paid no attention; they just danced out of reach. Their mothers would belt them before bedtime, but they would cook their dinners, too, and pull the covers up over them; and the kids knew that none of their badness would change that.

Those squares he'd seen in the subway today—the thought of them stuck in his throat and nearly choked him.

They thought they knew everything, just because they'd read a few books and seen a few programs. But what did they know about living? About staying alive on your own? Finding food for yourself when you were hungry? Getting cold and sleeping on the roof through the endless night—and then seeing the sun come again?

Those kids needed help for everything they did, and the whole world seemed willing to help them: mothers, teachers, cops, storekeepers, judges, and train conductors were on their side. But they couldn't even go around the block without asking someone's permission.

Even Dobbs Henry. "Wish we'd took them tickets

Mr. Levy was trying to give us." Thank *you*, Mr. Levy. James had never been able to forget what had happened with Timmie. Mr. Levy trying to help Timmie after turning him in in the first place. But the court wouldn't go along with Mr. Levy's being responsible for Timmie, and Timmie said he wouldn't have been no lousy stooge's stooge, anyway.

After the explosion, James thought Mr. Levy would turn him in, too; but he didn't. So James didn't have to turn down being probated to Mr. Levy, but he would have.

Mr. Levy pretending nothing had happened, and always asked about Timmie. But that was because Timmie was smart. All the other teachers remembered him, too. "How's your brother, James?" "Wish he hadn't dropped out." "Say hello to Timmie for me. Tell him to come in and see me. I might be able to find a job for him."

But Timmie only laughed at the messages. Timmie was too smart to get trapped in somebody else's plan.

But what if he got trapped in his own? That was what James kept worrying over.

Where was Timmie now? James felt a prickling under his skin. Timmie hadn't wanted to talk to him that afternoon; hadn't wanted him around. What did that mean?

James decided to try the ball park that belonged to

the parochial school. Sometimes Timmie's gang hid out there.

James turned the corner. The ball park was right in front of him, the street light making white bars of the seats. But the place wasn't empty. Shadows scurried across. Then there was the report of a gun, a crash, a tinkle of glass, and darkness.

A bright blot on his vision where the street light had been confused him more than the darkness, but left over in his mind was the impression of a silent line of figures streaking down the sidewalk.

James had to catch up. He spurted after them, running on the balls of his feet, noiselessly, and breathing with light, short gasps. The cops mustn't hear him.

But someone had heard him.

"Stop! Stop or we'll shoot!"

A tattoo of running steps was beating nearer and nearer.

James kept running. If he kept running, they said, they would shoot. And they would shoot. Just a few steps more, and it would happen. They would shoot and likely they'd hit him.

But what could he do? They were chasing, and he had to run.

"Stop running! We see you! You can't get away! We saw you come out of that liquor store! Kid, listen to me; you gotta stop running, or we'll have to shoot!"

That was funny. They had to chase him because they'd seen him running, and he had to run because they were chasing him. They had to shoot if he didn't stop, and he couldn't stop because they had to shoot. Nobody could keep it from happening.

The liquor store. Tim. Wanted to leave James out of it. James sensed that and followed. Had to be in with his brother.

James gave a great lunge toward the bleachers. One shot. His legs seemed caught in mid-stride like a slow motion film. One more shot. A broken-off yell fighting loose from his throat. He pitched forward and crashed.

Then, nothing.

american, too

JENNIFER SAW IT in the paper.

"Mama!" she cried out.

"What is it, darling?" asked Mama, leaning up on her elbow on the sofa. "What do you see there? Why do you speak in that tone?" A look of alarm haunted her thin face.

"Nothing," said Jennifer. "I mean, I see that it's going to be rainy tomorrow, Mama."

She mustn't give Mama another excuse for feeling gloomy!

More easily said than done.

"Ach, rain! Then Rosa can't hang the wash out in the sun to bleach, and it's the fourth bad washday this month," said Mama.

"But it's good for the flowers and crops, Mama," said Jennifer.

"Plenty of rain we've had already," Mama groaned. "Sun is what we need now, and no sun in the sky! It's vanished out of the universe!" Mama's marvelous rich quivering voice made everything she said into a proclamation, a reminder of past sorrows and announcement of more to come.

Jennifer usually went on trying to cheer Mama up for absolute ages, but this time she was too much upset. She couldn't help saying, "Well, maybe it isn't him, but I'm afraid I just know it is."

James Jonathon Purdy. James—that was what the other one had called him. Jonathon. A second name surprised her; a second name seemed to suggest that he had a mother who was interested in him; a second name was something extra, for luck. And Jonathon was such a brave kind of name. To look at James, you wouldn't certainly think him a coward, but Jonathon was a prince's name. His mother had to have known that. She must not be around any more. Nor anyone else who would like having a little fun with him, calling him Jimmy, or Jim. (If Dad were still alive, she, Jennifer, would still be Jenny.)

Her mother had been scanning her face, alarm deepening. "Who, darling? What's the matter? I knew it wasn't just rain!"

Mama was bolt upright now, breathing hard from her emphysema, her thin black brows pulled together.

(Jenny, you must not worry Mama. She starved, she suffered, she'll never be well, but we can keep from worrying her.)

Not today, Jenny couldn't.

"Well, Mama, this boy. See, here's his picture. They say he was critically injured when the police fired on some boys who'd been robbing a liquor store. They say he really wasn't involved; the other boys cleared him. One was his brother."

"A *Shwartsa!*" exclaimed Mama, looking at the picture. She folded her arms across her chest and rocked back and forth. "I don't understand the black people very well, they seem like children to me, but when I see what happens to them, oh, I feel it all again! The sound of marching boots while you huddle behind your door, waiting and waiting. The glare of hatred that sees itself instead of you. People tortured before your eyes. Again, and again, and again it can happen!"

"Mama, I saw this boy on the subway last Saturday. I told you I got to talking to a lot of kids who were going to that TV show? This one happened to be in our car, though he wasn't going, and he talked to us a little."

"You should never talk to strangers, especially those rough ones," said Mama. "But that this bad thing should happen to someone you know—for this

I am sorry. It's so bad when you know them. Like for me; you think I should forget? No, no, how can I forget? It was not just someone I knew; it was my mother! My father! My brother! And I should forget?"

"I know, Mama, but it's all over."

"All over! All over, she says! How do you know, all over? Look at the past! Whenever the Jews seem to prosper, whenever they say, 'It's all over, thank God,' it's only the sign that a new time is coming! And a worse!"

"No, Mama, no, Mama. It won't happen this time."

"But how can you know? In Germany, before the war, you would have said the same thing. Better than ever, we said! Who was great? Who was rich? Who was gay? Who won Nobel prizes, eleven in a row, more than anyone else? And then—then—"

"I know, Mama, I know," said Jennifer. Mama just had to get it all out of her system over again. It was as if she felt a duty not to let Jennifer forget, not to let herself get over it.

"Six million died, darling, six million people! Died, did you hear me? But not just died. Insulted, they were, hated, harried, and tortured. Your grandmother darling, your grandfather, and your poor little uncle, who never had time to do any good, or evil either!"

"Please, Mama! Please don't!"

Mama was sobbing now and rocking harder than ever. "What can you do? What can you do?"

Jennifer said quietly, "Let's have dinner. And we'll light the candles and say the prayers."

"The candles," mourned her mother, "the prayers. The little things that we carry through the world and the centuries on our back. So heavy, sometimes."

"They're not heavy, they're nice."

Later, when they were eating the lovely warm challah, Jennifer said, "I like being Jewish. And I like being English, from Daddy, and German from you, and Spanish, from my great-grandparents, and Jewish from Abraham and Moses. I like being part of Israel, forever and ever. And American too!"

"American you feel, then, too, darling? Along with all the rest?"

"Of course," said Jennifer. She thought of Rita and Tommy, her friends; and of Miss Bardon, her favorite teacher; and of the Hudson River, blue and dreamy between the bluffs and widening to a sea at the Tappan Zee Bridge. And she thought of the tall, deep-eyed man who had spoken the Gettysburg Address; and of President Kennedy's confident words: "Ask not what your country can do for you, ask what you can do for your country."

She picked up the paper and looked again at the picture of James, lying against the ambulance pillow, in a cap of bandages, his high-arched nose and closed eyes, still looking proud, though he was bound, broken, and helpless.

"Again, and again, and again it can happen."

Unless people who understood saw that it didn't.

"I have to be American," Jennifer said.

cecilia
wherever-you-are

THE WELFARE INVESTIGATOR had said to Cecilia, "Don't worry about anything. Everything's going to be all right."

And she'd added in a different tone to the Foster Mother, "It's true, you know. We generally neglect people shamefully, but when we find a nice needy family like this one, and get Special Agency to work on it, we do everything for them."

And that was really true, Cecilia thought, giving her dish towel a vicious crack. They had been doing everything for this nice, needy family.

So now Papa was in the hospital, and would go from there to the rehabilitation facility (Cecilia had learned a lot of impressive new words), and maybe get as well as ever. And Mama was in a special facility, too, for psychiatric treatment, so she wouldn't be so frightened and lonely. Cecilia could go and visit her in two more weeks. And Dominga was in yet another hospital, where they were going to fix her foot so it wouldn't turn sideways any longer. And Dolores and Cecilia were staying with this "nice foster-family," because there wasn't anything wrong with them that needed to be fixed in a hospital.

They only had to have someone to take care of them. So the Special Agency had referred them to a "private agency"—another phrase Cecilia had learned, which meant waiting for hours in offices and answering hundreds of questions. The private agency was a Foster Home Agency, and there weren't any foster homes near where the Lopezes had been living, so the girls had to go miles and miles and miles, over the East River and past Brooklyn and Queens and clear out on Long Island to Central Islip. This was a perfect place for them—a family that had come from Puerto Rico some time ago, who while they understood the Spanish language and Spanish ways, were "fully acculturated"—that is, had a car and a house in the suburbs.

"Have you got the dishes done yet, Cecilia?" asked Mrs. Ramirez, the nice foster mother.

"Yes," said Cecilia, hanging up the dish towel neatly.

Mrs. Ramirez gave her a pat. She *was* a nice foster mother. It was just that it was so far away from home, and everything was so different, and then, too, Cecilia couldn't act right.

She couldn't relax like Dolores. Right now, Dolores was playing jacks on the floor with six-year-old Billy. When that was over, she'd probably start playing Old Maid with ten-year-old Marty. Twelve-year-old Esteban (the only one who had been born in Puerto Rico, so he had a Spanish name) didn't have much to do with Dolores, and he didn't have much to do with Cecilia, either. And she didn't have anything to do with him.

"Do you have some homework tonight, Cecilia?" asked Mrs. Ramirez.

"Yes, ma'am," said Cecilia, and started up the stairs to the room which had been fixed up so nice in the attic of the little house and where she and Dolores slept.

"I didn't mean you had to run right upstairs, right after dinner, right after your chores," Mrs. Ramirez called after her. "Oh, dear. Well, all right, but come back down when you're through."

The bedroom was nice. The ceiling sloped down on each side, like a tent, and the two little beds sat cosily side by side at the end. The beds had flowered spreads, and the windows had ruffled curtains. There were two chests of drawers and a desk and a bookcase. It was a beautiful room.

Cecilia sat down at the desk and looked at the book she'd brought home from school. It was Friday night, and she had plenty of time to read the story. Though, of course, school was different out here. Classes were smaller, and most of the pupils were Anglos who read more easily in English than Spanish pupils usually could. So Cecilia had to work hard to keep up.

Outdoors it was dark and quiet. No tall lighted buildings or ˙neon signs, no cars going by; nobody yelling in the street; nobody fighting in the next apartment, nobody dancing upstairs, nobody pounding downstairs.

There was a noise downstairs, though, the busy mumbling voice of the TV in the living room. Then boxed laughter, then music, then silence, then family laughter. Cecilia could hear Dolores's voice mingling in with the rest.

Cecilia sat still and longed to join them. She pictured it a dozen times: she would go downstairs, open the door at the foot of the steps, tiptoe down the little hall, slip in behind them while they were all staring at the screen, and drop on the floor beside Dolores. Mrs. Ramirez would look over at her and smile and say, "Oh, good, Cecilia!"

There wasn't any reason why she shouldn't do this. *No* reason.

Now she heard Billy's voice, raised in furious disagreement, as usual.

"I won't go to bed yet!" said Billy. "I'm not going! You said I could stay up an hour extra with Dolores!"

Low murmurs from his mother.

"NO!" yelled Billy. "That's not fair! You can't make me!"

Cecilia could not believe how bad Billy was. His mother never told him to do anything but what was right. And he never did it. He refused, argued, whined, groaned, and pleaded. Mrs. Ramirez just sighed and groaned herself, and laughed a little, and sometimes let it go, and sometimes suddenly reached over and gave Billy a slap.

Evidently that was what she did now. Or maybe Mr. Ramirez leaped out of his newspaper and did it for her. Anyway, there was a sudden pause, then a bellow from Billy, which died away in a lessening volley of hiccuping sobs.

After five days of experience, Cecilia was able to picture Mrs. Ramirez picking up the dangle-legged boy and carrying him into his room, where she would act out the long ritual of reading stories and singing songs, to make up to him for—what? Cecilia couldn't imagine.

Anyway, it spoiled her plan of going downstairs. Mrs. Ramirez was her only port. Mr. Ramirez was silent and black-browed. She didn't dare speak to him.

Marty was silly, and Esteban—oh, she was a hundred times more afraid of him than of Mr. Ramirez. Esteban was so wonderful! He was serious and intelligent and obeyed his parents, but he could sing and make jokes, too. What a brother he would have been! But he didn't even notice her.

So, after a while, she went to bed. That was just awful, because she couldn't go to sleep, and she kept wondering how Papa was, trying to believe it was true what the investigator had told her about his being out of danger and sure to get well. And she worried about Mama, off by herself and *locked up*—at least, Cecilia supposed she was locked up, for that was the only way they could have made her stay away from her family. And about Dominga, at the end of the long corridor in a room with many other young children in cribs. Dominga would have to go through frightening and painful experiences that she wouldn't understand. Of course, she would have more toys and children of her own age to play with than ever before. When Cecilia left, with the welfare lady, on Sunday, and looked back to wave goodbye, Dominga had forgotten all about her in a game of hide and seek between the crib bars with the child in the next bed.

Her fears about Dominga were that Dominga would forget them.

Cecilia slept a little and was wakened by Dolores

coming in and turning on the light.

"Why didn't you come down?" asked Dolores. "We saw a good movie, and Mrs. Ramirez fixed some popcorn."

Cecilia didn't answer.

"I wonder how Papa and Mama and Dominga are," she said through the darkness when Dolores had hopped into bed.

"O.K., I guess. Why wouldn't they be?"

And in another minute, Dolores was asleep. But Cecilia couldn't go to sleep again for a long time.

Saturday. Their first Saturday with the Ramirezes. Nobody waked them up, but Cecilia got up just the same as usual, and made her bed, and went downstairs. Nobody was around. She sat and looked at a magazine. She got up and peeked out the window. The back yard was full of grass, neat and smooth. And cold and empty.

Cecilia went back upstairs. Dolores was still asleep. Cecilia went down again. She noiselessly collected the popcorn dishes and washed them.

She had just started to sweep the messy living room when Mrs. Ramirez came in, yawning, in her bathrobe.

"I thought I heard somebody prowling around," said Mrs. Ramirez. "My goodness, can't you ever stop working?"

She started the coffeepot and cooked bacon and toast. Billy came out in his pajamas and stood at the foot of the stairs.

"Dolores!" he roared.

"Billy, you keep quiet! Let her finish her sleep," admonished his mother.

"Dolores!" bawled Billy, louder if anything.

"Just a little minute!" Dolores called down sleepily in Spanish.

Shortly afterward, Esteban came into the living room and began to tune in the TV.

"Want some breakfast, honey?" called his mother from the kitchen.

"Naw," said Esteban. "It's time for my program. Thanks, I'll get it later."

Cecilia's heart beat faster. It was almost eleven. That was the time for Science Searchlight. Could it be—?

It was. There was the familiar studio, the backdrop of night sky with planets, the table with its paraphernalia for demonstrations. There was Tom Degen. The program started.

Why it was, Cecilia didn't know, but this world of science was somehow more real to her than the world of people, where most things seemed to happen without meaning, uncomfortably, or calamitously. She forgot everything else in watching, until the station break, when Esteban went to the kitchen and came back with a glass of milk and a doughnut. Noticing Cecilia, he stopped short, stared helplessly, and gave a gesture with the doughnut as if to say, "Oh, you still here? Well—want one?"

Cecilia gave a half-shake of her head; he had only half asked her, so she could only half refuse. He'd *noticed* her, anyway.

The second half of the program was as interesting as the first, only shorter.

"I see our time is almost over," said Tom Degen. "As usual, I want to introduce some of the interesting people in the studio audience. Sometimes I introduce famous scientists, other times a group who have come from far away. Today, I think it's the most unusual group who has ever come to our program. They're school kids, using the tickets we distribute, like so many others, but—they're different."

Cecilia gave a gasp. Esteban looked to see what was wrong with her.

"They're not 'a group from the Bronx,' like I sometimes tell you about; they're not 'some Westchester County Seventh-graders,' or 'a class from PS Such-and-Such in Harlem.' They're from all over the lot—Bronx, Westchester, *and* Harlem, and they're not a class, or even a group. But they're not just separate individuals, either. Listen to their story, and you'll

know what I mean."

Could it be, Cecilia wondered, *could* it be?

"Last Saturday morning," Tom Degen went on dramatically, "a lot of separate youngsters started downtown on the subway. They were from different schools and from different lives. . ."

He went on and told it, and while he told, the camera swung slowly back and forth over the faces of the group. Cecilia stared with her mouth open. There was Hal, serious and unflinching; Susan, biting her lip to keep from laughing; a Negro boy Cecilia didn't think she had seen before; Jennifer, absorbedly twisting a long strand of hair around her finger; Terry, making side remarks to that thin boy, John Something, who knew so much; and the round-faced Harlem boy, who kept looking up and talking to a tall dark man who grinned back at him.

"Now I'm going to ask them to tell their names and where they come from," said Tom Degen, "but not their own names. Each one can introduce the next one. Hal, you start. This is Hal Hunter, from White Plains."

Hal introduced the strange Negro boy next to him. "This is Franklin Wyatt. He might be a scientist someday. He's from our school. He wasn't with us last week, but he will be from now on."

Franklin introduced Susan. "She don't know much, but she's learning."

Susan stuck out her tongue at him. "This is Jennifer. She was the one who had the idea of our coming together this week."

Jennifer got up. "I don't think it was I who thought of it, I think it was Terry. Terry McIlvane."

Terry shook his head. "No, it was Hal. Guess we all thought of it, though. This is John. He's the one guy who really knows about this Science stuff."

John introduced Dobbs Henry, cracking his knuckles as he did so.

Dobbs Henry wrinkled up his nose and looked first one way and then the other, as if he were hunting an escape. Finally he closed his eyes. He didn't say a word. Everyone was laughing. So the man beside him got up and said, "Dobbs Henry was on the train last week, but he didn't have a ticket to the program. This week he wanted to come, and he let me come with him. I'm Stephen Levy, his teacher."

Cecilia let out her breath in an explosive sigh. If only she could call out, "And here am I, Cecilia!" She couldn't even get up courage to say to Esteban, "I know them! I was there!"

Then the camera swung again. It focussed on Jennifer. Jennifer was standing up. She threw her hair back over her shoulders.

"Jennifer has asked if she can say something special."

Jennifer nodded, the light flashing off her glasses.

"Well," she said, "you see, there were two more kids with us who aren't here today. We know where one of them is. James! James Jonathon Purdy in the hospital, we're thinking of you! We wish you were here, and hope you feel better now. The other person disappeared and didn't come back. We wish she were with us, too, and we hope she'll come next week. Hello, Cecilia, wherever you are!"

Laughter, clapping, and abruptly, it was all over, and the commercial had come on.

"Cecilia!" repeated Esteban, "Why, that's your name!"

Cecilia blushed but looked straight at him. "It was me."

"You went down there by yourself?"

Cecilia nodded.

"You're interested in science?"

Cecilia nodded.

"You were in that subway tie-up with all those kids?"

Cecilia nodded.

Esteban began fiddling with the TV, snapping it from channel to channel. Finally he turned it off and looked round at Cecilia.

"I think I'll go down to the studio next week and see that program. We can get tickets at our school, too. I always kinda wanted to go. Want to go along?"

Cecilia nodded.

out of the tunnel

NIGHT IN THE HOSPITAL is a long dark tunnel.

The clanging ambulance, the flashing red lights, the stretcher, shifting insecurely as it is balanced between a tall man and a short man going up steps, the drone of an elevator, and the painful transfer of an aching body to the bed.

And then the tunnel.

James thought confusedly that he must be in the Tunnel of Mystery at the amusement park. He was shooting along, on his back, but headfirst, through smothery rubber darkness. Then he turned a corner and came out on a bright crazy scene.

Some woman was shouting, "Open your mouth! Wider! Don't bite!"

Her white clothing crackled like paper as she bent over to poke a thermometer into his mouth. She took it out, looked at it, shook it, and suddenly the scene blotted out as she creaked away.

Then miles and miles more of tunnel, the furtive, soft movement of his passage turning his stomach over. Even though he was tired and sick, he couldn't rest, for there was something he had to do. But what was it?

Finally he did go to sleep, and when he woke up it was daytime. Light flooded through windows, over white beds, tables, and pale-green walls. In the bed nearest him a boy lay with his leg suspended in a kind of sling. He was weaving something on a frame.

"Good," said a voice above him, "you're coming out of it. Take a little of this." Blue eyes were looking down at him out of a pink face. A glass straw slid into his mouth, the other end crooked into a glass. He pushed his end out with his tongue and tried to sit up. Wow! His head began to whirl, and the sickness came boiling up again. He dropped back on his pillow.

"You're not up to jumping around much, yet," said the nurse. "You had a concussion. And your leg is pretty sore; the bone wasn't broken, but it's a pretty deep gash."

She lifted the covers and showed him a great oblong package that seemed to be connected onto him. It hurt him to try to move it.

"But you'll be O.K. pretty soon. Go back to sleep."

And she went to the next bed.

James lay and stared at the ceiling. He remembered, now. He had been hunting for Timmie, and then the cops shot him up. Was he in jail? And what had happened to Timmie?

His thoughts couldn't get any farther, so he went to sleep again. He struggled through another feverish night into another bright day.

His head was clearer now, and he could see that he wasn't in jail, but in a hospital.

"Well, hi!" said the pink-faced nurse, offering him the glass tube again. "You're better today."

But he didn't feel any better. He shoved the glass tube away again.

If the night was a tunnel, the day was a cage. Nurses and doctors came and went, glancing at him as if he were part of the furniture. He couldn't do a thing. He was trapped. No wonder the bears in the zoo paced back and forth and then stood swaying in despair. They knew it wouldn't help them get away, but they had to do something just to keep from going crazy.

There wasn't even that much for James; he couldn't even sway. So he concentrated on stillness. He looked at the ceiling.

If he could only find out what had happened to Timmie, and what they were going to do to *him*. Put him in jail, when he was patched up enough? Timmie might be in jail now, or he might have got away. Or even—what if they'd shot Timmie, too? What if—? There was no way of knowing. James couldn't possibly ask; asking might give Timmie away.

That is, he couldn't ask any of these strangers, and who else was there? This weird new life was entirely disconnected from the old. Nobody he knew would ever get over from one to the other. Naomi hated hospitals, ever since her baby died in one. If Dobbs Henry ever saw a hospital to recognize it, he'd run in the other direction. Nobody would come here to see James and tell him what had happened. He was stuck, that was all.

"You've got to eat, you know, or you won't get well," said the pink-faced nurse.

Why should he want to get well?

"All right, we'll feed him intravenously," said the doctor, who wasn't as gentle as the nurse. He was cross. "More trouble than you're worth, Buster."

They poked the needle into his arm and bound it to a tube that led a steady flow of liquid from a suspended bottle. The tickling trickle drove him crazy. He thrashed his arm around until the tube pulled off.

When the nurse came on her night rounds, she noticed it was disconnected. She didn't say anything, just went out quickly. Probably the doctor or some nurse-boss would come and lay him out for fair.

She did bring back another nurse—dark-skinned, with smooth, rounded features. The new one had a little gold pin on her collar. She was older, and moved like a head lady. She stood above the bed gazing down at him thoughtfully, then dismissed the other nurse with a little jerk of her head. But still she didn't speak, just waited.

That was a game that always worked. James played it himself. But this lady could carry it further than he —at least, here, on her own ground, she could.

"Well, say something!" he growled feebly.

She smiled. "How do you feel?"

He answered, defiantly but frankly, "Out of it! I don't know which way's up."

She got a little excited at that, and leaned out of her queen-pose.

"Nobody's told you what happened! I thought they'd have told you downstairs. Well, *I'll* tell you. They caught up with your brother and the rest of the boys, who told them you had nothing to do with the robbery."

"Was they hurt?"

"No, but they'll have to appear in court soon. I'm afraid they'll have it pretty hard. They're over eighteen and have been on the books before, you know."

James was so relieved he hardly heard the last part. Two things had been bugging him: would they think he'd been in on it, and had Timmie been hurt or killed. Jail? Oh, sure. At Timmie's age, you kind of took that for granted.

He slept fourteen hours.

"Ready for some chow?" asked the pink-faced nurse when he opened his eyes. She put the tray down on the table. He stared greedily as she lifted the silver covers. Soup! Phooey. Jello! Double phooey.

"Can't I have anything to *eat?*" he groaned.

"Look what I got!" crowed the boy in the next bed. "Chicken and french fries!"

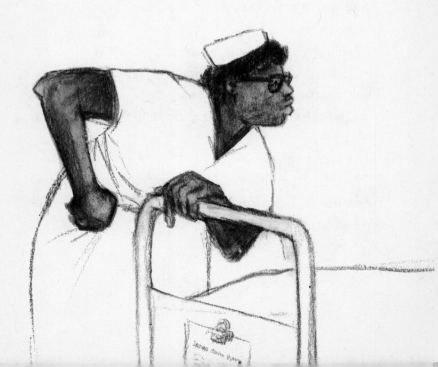

Life in the hospital soon began to seem better. There was plenty going on. The boy in the next bed was willing to tell everything about himself and his family and his whole life. He was also very curious about James. James let him chatter all he wanted, but gave out only very short and uninformative replies to the questions.

But when the trays came, and Walter (that was his name) lifted the silver covers off his well-filled steaming dishes of meat and potatoes and pie, it did much to even the score. Also, Walter had the best of it at visiting hours. Father, mother, aunts, uncles, grandparents, minister, and friends of the family visited

him. And they all brought presents.

By evening of the third day, James felt almost himself again, provided he didn't move too quickly. The hospital rat-race was so familiar he felt as if he'd been there always. Katy, the pink-faced nurse, was O.K. Even the crabby old doctor, he found, always had a mustardy joke hidden in his bawling out. And there was all kinds of stuff going on all the time. Walter told him stories about kids who had been in the room before he came; Walter was having skin grafts, and had been there a long time. Katy told them about a guy down the hall who'd got stepped on by an elephant!

You never knew what was going to happen next. Of course, it was mostly accidents, and not too pleasant; but it was exciting.

On the fourth day, Katy lifted the silver covers with a flourish: bacon and eggs and pancakes!

But still the visitors bothered him. They came eagerly stampeding down the hall at two o'clock. They parked around the door of the rooms across the hall. They surrounded Walter's bed.

They were always saying, "When you come home."

"When you come home, you can sleep downstairs in the sunroom so you won't have to climb steps."

"When you come home, I'll make apple pie and

chocolate cake every day!"

"When you come home, Daddy says he's going to get you that puppy, for sure."

Whereas, when James went home . . .

On the fifth day, the social worker came to see him. He stared her up and down.

"I don't need no investigator. My sister'll look after me."

She said nothing, only tipped her head dubiously and shook it. Naomi must have told the social worker she wouldn't.

"Or my Aunt Tony Benton."

"How would you like to go to a nice foster home?" she asked.

"Fleas to your nice foster home," said James, and the social worker left.

"You shouldn't have talked to her like that," said Katy when she brought him his dinner. "She could help you. What are you going to do when you get out of here?"

That was a good question.

He decided he wouldn't leave, he wouldn't get well. But on Monday the doctor examined him and grunted, "You're about as good as new—however good that is." It was a joke, but James couldn't appreciate it.

Of course, he didn't want to be sick forever and

stay in this cage, even if it was a comfortable one. But the outside—especially with Timmie in jail—looked pretty awful. The social work lady of course would get him in the end.

It was visiting hours again. That dreaded time.

"Wash your face," said Katy.

"Why should I?" grumbled James.

And then he saw somebody at the door. A tall, thin, dark-haired man hesitated there, a box of candy in his hand,—a hand with a scar.

Peeking around him like a chipmunk, curious and round-eyed, was Dobbs Henry.

It was something James had been waiting for, without knowing it, for a long time.

"Katy," said James. "Them guys is for me."